Snow Dogs

by

Jane A. C. West

Illustrated by Dylan Gibson

To the Nowzad Dogs – and all the four-legged friends who have changed my life

You do not need to read this page – just get on with the book!

First published in 2008 in Great Britain by
Barrington Stoke Ltd
18 Walker St, Edinburgh, EH3 7LP

www.barringtonstoke.co.uk

ISBN: 978-1-84299-560-0

Printed in Great Britain by Bell & Bain Ltd

 Scottish **Arts** Council

Contents

Chapter 1
The Iditarod

A cold, wet nose pressed Zeb's cheek.

"Get off, Nukka!" said Zeb.

Nukka wagged her tail. She was happy. She was Zeb's best husky dog and she knew it. She could get away with a lot.

Zeb got Nukka when she was a puppy. She liked to poke her nose into everything. She liked to boss the other dogs. Nukka means "little sister". She made Zeb think of a cheeky little sister who chased him around all day. She never got tired.

Zeb was 15. He lived in Anchorage, a small town in Alaska. Alaska is the part of the USA that sticks out, next to Canada – it's a cold place.

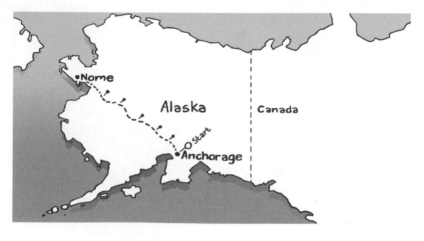

There are two main sports in Alaska, ice hockey and dog sledding. Zeb didn't like hockey but he loved dog sledding. When the sky was blue and the air was cold, going sledding was the best thing in the world.

Zeb had eight dogs to pull his sled and he rode behind them. He stood on the sled. Nukka was the lead dog out in front.

Years ago, in the days before they had cars and snow-mobiles, dog sledding was not just a sport. It was the only way of getting round on snow and ice. There are still times when you need to use sleds. In 1925, hundreds of people in the town of Nome got sick. They needed medicine fast, but no car could drive over the snow and frozen ice, so

they had to use sleds. Men and dogs had to
bring medicine 674 miles by sled back to
Nome. They saved hundreds of lives.

Zeb had been told that story since he
was a baby.

"We could do that easy, Nukka," said Zeb.

Nukka wagged her tail. "We could do more than that."

Zeb's dream was to race his dogs on the Iditarod trail, the hardest dog race in the world. It was 1,149 miles across snow and ice. It was you and your dogs against the cold and ice. Alone.

The race was run to remember how the people of Nome were saved in 1925. The man who won the Iditarod was a hero.

"The prize money could buy Mum and Dad a nice house," said Zeb to Nukka.

He was fed up with just dreaming.

Chapter 2
Just a Kid

The Iditarod race took place every March. Four days before the race began men and dogs from other parts of Alaska and Canada and from places all over the world came to Zeb's home town of Anchorage.

The men who drove the dog sleds were called 'mushers'. The name comes from the word 'mush' which means 'go' in husky-speak. Having your own words shows you are different from other people. 'Gee' means 'go right' and 'haw' means 'go left'. 'Whoa' is 'slow down'.

Zeb was proud to be such a young musher. He was good at it.

Zeb and his dad watched the other mushers arrive.

"Look, Dad! There's Martin Buser. He won twice in 1992 and 1994. I thought he'd stopped racing."

"I don't think old mushers ever stop racing," said Zeb's dad. "They just slide away."

"Ha, ha! That's funny, Dad. Don't you mean sled away!"

Zeb waited a moment then said, "Dad, can I ..."

"I know what you're going to say, Zeb. But I still say no. You're too young. You have to be 18 to race in the Iditarod. You're only 15 now. In three years we'll talk about it again."

"But, Dad ..."

"I said no."

Zeb's dad walked away.

Zeb felt angry. He was just as good as these mushers – better.

"I could do the Iditarod now!" he yelled.

An old musher with a long, white beard shook his head. "Son, this race ain't for kids. It's hard. Real hard. You get it wrong and you die."

Another musher came over.

"You listen to the old man, kid. This race isn't for babies. It's for real men. Stay home and do what your mum tells you."

Zeb's face was red as he walked away.

"I'll show them," he said to himself. "I'll show them all."

Chapter 3
The First Mistake

That night Zeb made up his mind he would enter the Iditarod – no matter what anyone said.

"I'm not a kid. I'm as good as any of them."

He took his ID card and turned '15' into '18'. It was easy. "Now they'll have to let me race," he said to himself.

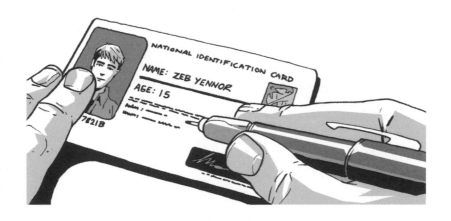

There was a lot to do before the race started. Zeb looked at the long list of things he needed:

Food for 3 weeks

Dog food for 8 dogs

Warm clothes

Sun glasses

Mini stove with fuel

Matches

Radio

Water

Sleeping bag

Tent

Rifle and bullets.

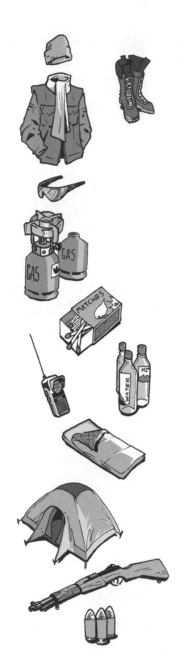

The list went on.

"And I mustn't forget the 32 booties."

These booties weren't for Zeb. Each dog needed a set of 4 to cover its paws. Sharp ice could cut a dog's paws badly.

"I'll have to hide all this or Mum and Dad will find it. No way would they let me race – or even leave the house."

Zeb had three days to make his plan work.

He hid his food and other things in a shed behind the house. No one went in there. It was full of old rubbish. He'd be safe.

But the night before the race, Zeb was thinking about how his parents would feel when they found he'd gone.

"I'd better leave a note for Mum and Dad. Once I'm on the trail they can't stop me, but I don't want them to worry."

Zeb wrote this note to his parents.

Dear Mum and Dad
You'll sure be shocked when you know where I've gone! I'm doing the Iditarod! Don't worry - Nukka will look after me. I promise I'll be safe and I'll be home soon.
Please don't be cross - I know I can do this.
Love,
Zeb

The next morning, he left the note on his bed.

"By the time they read this, I'll be gone," he said.

But when he closed his bedroom door, the note was blown off the bed. It fell onto a pile of mags under the bed. Zeb's parents never saw it.

Chapter 4
An Angry Moose

The man looked at Zeb's ID.

"Are you sure you're 18, son?"

"Yes!" said Zeb. "Ten weeks ago."

"And you've got all the stuff on the list? Your sled looks a bit light."

"I've got everything I need."

The man shook his head. "I can't stop you, son. If you have any problems, use your radio. OK?"

Zeb grinned. "I won't have any problems."

The man shook his head again and told Zeb to go to the start line.

Over 70 mushers and their dogs waited side by side at the start line.

"If Mum and Dad are here, they'll never see me in this crowd," said Zeb. He felt a bit bad about his mum and dad, but he'd see them again soon.

The race began and the mushers set off. They went slowly at the start. But as they left the town behind, before them was nothing but a world of white. Zeb's dogs picked up speed and ran through the snow. They loved this as much as he did.

Zeb's fast team and light sled flew over the snow. He was in the lead!

The trail took Zeb into the silent forest. The sled and the dogs sounded loud. Nukka turned her head left and right. It was hard for her to see in the dim light.

"What's the matter, Nukka?" said Zeb.

She gave a bark to warn him.

Out of the forest came a large moose. A male with big, sharp antlers.

Zeb knew that a male moose was very heavy, he could weigh over 1,500 pounds. And an angry moose could run up to 35 miles an hour. If the antlers didn't get you, a kick from one of its hooves could kill.

This one wasn't happy to see them. It was hungry after a long winter, and it was in a bad temper. The moose hated people and hated wolves. To the moose, Zeb's dogs looked like wolves.

A grown man weighs 150 pounds. And adult moose weighs the same as ten men. 1,500 pounds. The angry moose charged at Zeb.

"Mush! Mush!" yelled Zeb.

Nukka knew what to do. She turned away from the moose, and was soon running at top speed. The other dogs ran too. Fear made them fast.

The moose's angry bellow rang behind them.

The dogs ran and ran until the moose was out of sight.

"That was a bit too close," said Zeb, his voice shaking. "Thanks, Nukka."

Chapter 5
Ice Storm

The race was going well. In the last two weeks Zeb and his dogs had covered over 1,000 miles of snow and ice. The days were happy and full of joy. He spent the nights in cosy cabins with the dogs.

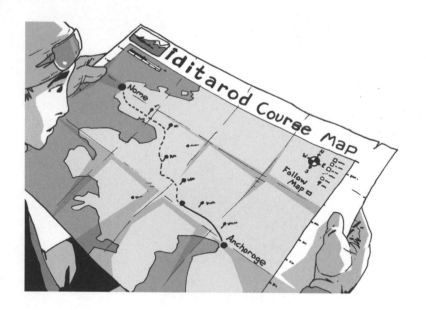

This morning Zeb woke up and stretched.
He could see his breath in the cold morning
air. Nukka stuck her nose into his pocket
looking for a treat. Zeb stroked her thick
fur.

"Sorry, Nukka. I haven't got any treats.
We're getting a bit low on food."

Nukka looked sad.

Today, the light was sharp and clear.
The dogs were running well, the sled ride
was smooth and fast.

This was what dog-sledding was all
about. A good team, a blue sky and the end
of the race just a few days away. No one as
young as Zeb had ever finished the Iditarod.

Zeb should have looked behind him.

A storm was coming. A smart musher
would make camp now, put up a tent and
shelter from the storm. Zeb had forgotten
the first rule of sledding – be ready.

Suddenly the wind was icy. Snow was
settling on the dogs' backs.

"I can't see the trail," said Zeb, feeling nervous.

The storm raged around them. Snow like steel cut into them. Zeb's dogs were running blind now. They were scared by the fierce storm. Mushers call it a 'white-out'. It was all Zeb could do to hold on to the sled. He could not feel his hands – his fingers were numb.

"If I fall off the sled," he said to himself, "I'll be dead."

In this weather, a man could freeze to death fast.

"I must stop the sled," said Zeb. "We could drive into a crevasse." A crevasse was like a big crack in the thick ice sheet – some were hundreds of feet deep. All mushers feared them. If you fell in, no one would ever find your body.

Shouting 'woah' wasn't going to stop the dogs now. Most days Zeb could shout 'woah' and press the foot brake to slow the sled. Not today. The dogs were in a panic. He would have to use the ice hook – a way of getting the dogs to turn or suddenly stop. "A bit like a hand-brake in a car," Zeb's dad had told him.

Zeb used all his muscles and slammed the iron hook into the icy ground with his left hand. The sled started to tip over and Zeb cried out. He threw himself to the right. "I must keep the sled up!"

Too late.

The heavy sled crashed down on its side and stopped. Zeb was thrown clear.

Nukka ran to Zeb and licked him with her pink tongue. He didn't move.

Water freezes at 0°C. At minus 44°C, skin freezes in less than a minute. Warm clothes keep you safe for up to half an hour. But no one was coming to help Zeb. He was on his own.

Chapter 6
Pain

The storm roared all day and all night. The dogs huddled around Zeb to keep him warm. Without the heat of their bodies, he would have frozen to death.

In the pale morning light, Zeb woke up. He groaned in pain and Nukka licked his face. She was worried for Zeb. He tried to

sit up but pain stabbed through him. It hurt
to breathe. Had he broken a rib, maybe two
or three?

"It's the end of the trail for us, Nukka,"
he said. "I must radio for help. My parents
are going to kill me."

Zeb stood up slowly. He was in great
pain. He swore and held his ribs. He pulled
the sled the right way up. He got the radio
out of his pack. His mouth went dry. The
radio was broken. Useless.

"This is really bad news," he said.

Nukka licked his hand.

Zeb had no choice. He had to go on.

He fed the dogs what little food was left. For himself, he opened a tin of beans. It was frozen solid and Zeb's mini stove had no fuel left.

He put the frozen tin of beans in his
pocket. He hoped the heat of his body would
melt them.

Zeb slowly got on the sled. He hurt all
over.

"Mush! Mush!" he yelled.

The dogs pulled hard and the sled moved off. Most times Zeb would help the dogs by running behind the sled. Today he rode the sled and the dogs had to work even harder to pull it. Zeb felt bad: bad for the dogs, bad for his parents, and bad for himself.

Zeb was hurt, out of food, out of fuel, with a broken radio and 200 miles of snow and ice to go before he got to the end of the race.

"It can't get any worse," he said to himself.

But it would.

Chapter 7
Love and Loss

The next two days were a night-mare. Zeb and his dogs were hungry and tired. Zeb clung to the sled. He felt pain with every breath.

At last, Zeb passed two empty log cabins in an hour. He was getting near Nome – the end of the race.

Zeb felt hope for the first time. They were going to make it!

Then Zeb felt the dogs getting slower. He was angry. Why were they stopping?

"Mush!" he yelled. "Come on, Nukka!"

But Nukka did not move. She growled softly.

Zeb looked up and felt sick.

A large polar bear was watching them.

Polar bears were often seen near Nome. They stole food and ate from dustbins. They also hunted and killed dogs. Sometimes they killed people. They were fast and deadly. They were born hunters, born killers. And they weren't afraid of men.

Zeb got his rifle and tried to load the bullets. His hands were shaking badly.

Nukka growled in fear and anger and then started to bark. The other dogs were in a panic. They tried to get away, but they were tied to the sled.

Then the polar bear charged.

Nukka snapped her tug-lines and sprang
at the bear. She was a big, strong dog –
over 130 pounds.

But the polar bear was 1,000 pounds and stood nine feet tall. The fight could not last for long.

The bear's long claws tore at Nukka. She yelped once. The snow turned red with her blood.

"Nooooo!" yelled Zeb. He fired his rifle at the bear. He knew the small bullets could not hurt the bear, but the noise would drive it away.

He walked towards the bear, firing shot after shot. He didn't care if he lived or died. He had to save Nukka.

The bear roared at Zeb as it backed away, then turned and ran.

Zeb raced to Nukka. Her eyes were closed but she was still alive. When he stroked her, Nukka's eyes opened and she licked his hand.

"Nukka! I'm sorry! Please don't die! We're nearly there! Hold on!"

Shaking and crying, Zeb put Nukka on the back of the sled.

The seven other dogs pulled hard and the sled began to move.

An hour later, they crossed the finish line in Nome. They weren't first, but no musher as young as Zeb had ever finished the Iditarod. A huge cheer went up from the crowd. Zeb saw his mum and dad running towards him.

"We knew we'd find you here!"

Then they saw the look on his face.

"Help Nukka," was all he could say.

Zeb's dad ran to the sled.

"I'm sorry, son," he said. "Nukka is dead."

Zeb got a hero's welcome from the people of Nome. But he didn't care. Nukka was gone.

Two days later, Zeb, his parents and the other dogs travelled back to Anchorage.

"Nukka gave her life for you," said Zeb's dad. "That's how much she loved you. You were all she cared about."

"If I hadn't done this stupid race, she'd still be alive," said Zeb.

Zeb's dad nodded. "I know. And you'll have to live with that forever. You'll never forget Nukka. She saved your life. Dogs are like that. Treat them well and they'll always be loyal."

He looked at Zeb. "Your mum and I thought this might make you feel better." He put a small box into Zeb's hands.

Curled up in a bed of straw was a tiny husky puppy. "She's called Buniq," said Zeb's dad. "It means 'sweet daughter'."

Zeb smiled with tears on his cheeks as he stroked the warm fur.

Barrington Stoke would like to thank all its readers for commenting on the manuscript before publication and in particular:

Tim Andrews

Scott Evison

Peter King

Ben Kirkwood

Frederick Lange

Alex Langton

Rachel Langton

Pieter Lap

Tommy Lee

Paul Maddon

Rebecca Metton

Dhena Patel

Harry Penrice

Kieron Skelton

Lea Smith

Freddie Stebbings

Giacomo Sumner

Laura Waugh

Become a Consultant!

Would you like to give us feedback on our titles before they are published? Contact us at the email address below – we'd love to hear from you!

info@barringtonstoke.co.uk
www.barringtonstoke.co.uk